Tilly's Pony Tails
Royal Flame
the police horse

D1321859

Pippa Funnell

Illustrated by Jennifer Miles

Orion
Children's Books

ORION CHILDREN'S BOOKS

First published in Great Britain in 2011
by Orion Children's Books
This new edition published in 2013
by Orion Children's Books
This edition published in 2016 by Hodder and Stoughton

7 9 10 8

A CIP catalogue record for this book
is available from the British Library.

ISBN 978 1 4440 0262 1

Printed and bound in Great Britain
by Clays Ltd, St Ives plc

The paper and board used in this book are
made from wood from responsible sources.

MIX
Paper from
responsible sources
FSC
www.fsc.org   FSC® C104740

Orion Children's Books
An imprint of
Hachette Children's Group
Part of Hodder and Stoughton
Carmelite House
50 Victoria Embankment
London EC4Y 0DZ

An Hachette UK Company
www.hachette.co.uk

www.hachettechildrens.co.uk

Tilly's Pony Tails

Royal Flame
the police horse

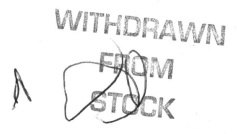

To Jenny Kleboe,
for all the endless hours of help over the years

Hello!

When I was little, I, like Tilly, was absolutely crazy about horses and ponies. All my books, pictures and toys had something to do with my four-legged friends.

I was lucky because a great friend of my mother's lent us a little woolly pony called Pepsi. He lived in the field at my best friend's house. I loved spending as much time as possible with him, but hated having to scrape all the mud off his shaggy winter coat. I used to lie in bed at night longing for the day I'd be able to have a smart horse all clipped and snuggled up in a stable with nice warm rugs.

My birthday treat every year was to go to The Horse of the Year Show, and

I remember going to Badminton and Burghley as a child. It was seeing top riders at these famous venues that gave me the inspiration to follow my dreams.

Now I've had the opportunity to ride some wonderful horses, all of whom have a special place in my heart. It's thanks to them that I have achieved my dreams and won so many competitions at the highest level. I still ride all day, every day, live, sleep and breathe horses and I love every minute of it.

Many of you will not be as used to horses as I am, so I have tried to include some of what I have learned in these books. At the back is a glossary so you can look up any unfamiliar words.

I hope you will enjoy reading the books in my series *Tilly's Pony Tails*, as much as I have enjoyed creating a girl who, like me, follows her passions. I hope that Tilly will inspire many readers to follow their dreams.

Love

One

It was a chilly winter's day. Tilly Redbrow adjusted her warm riding gloves and sat up straight in the saddle. She was having an early morning lesson at Silver Shoe Farm with her instructor, Angela. Tilly and her horse, Magic Spirit, were working on different types of trot.

'That's good Tilly. Now move into a medium trot. Remember, the rhythm and tempo remain the same as the working trot, but Magic has to cover more ground.

Longer, bigger steps, without increasing the speed.'

Tilly allowed Magic to extend his head and neck slightly. She kept a good contact with his mouth as she softened her arms forward. Gradually, the length

of Magic's steps increased as Tilly put more leg on.

'Great,' said Angela approvingly.

They did the steps across the diagonal of the sand school and were about to go again when Tilly caught sight of a magnificent bay horse in the distance, being led towards the yard. It wasn't a horse she knew, not a Silver Shoe regular. He was tall and sturdy, with a light copper red coat and black points.

'Stay focused, Tilly! You've lost the rhythm. The steps are irregular now. Magic's lost his balance.'

Tilly felt Magic speed up. They'd both lost concentration. Closing her legs and letting her seat sink deeper into the saddle, Tilly made a transition to halt.

Magic stopped immediately and Tilly walked him back to Angela.

'You were going so well. What happened?' said Angela, shaking her head and smiling.

'I got distracted,' said Tilly. 'It was my fault. Sorry, Magic.'

She leaned forward and patted his neck.

'You'll both have to learn to ignore distractions – think of all the things going on at a competition,' said Angela. 'I know you'd probably prefer to be jumping or out hacking, but flat work is the best way to improve your riding. It helps horses strengthen up so they become better educated, balanced and well-mannered. It's important to keep practising.'

'I know,' said Tilly. 'And I will practise, as much as I can. I want Magic and I to be the best we can be.'

'That's the right attitude. Well, I think we've done enough this morning, Tilly. It's very cold. Put a turn-out rug on Magic and take him down to the long field. Then I suggest you go and get a hot chocolate from the club room. Looks as though you could do with warming up.'

Tilly brushed a hand across her forehead and wiped frosty hairs from her eyes. She could see her breath in the air.

'Okay,' she said. 'Thanks for the lesson.'

'You're welcome,' said Angela. 'We'll have another one next week and work on the canter a bit more. See you later.'

As Tilly led Magic away from the sand school, she thought about the bay horse she'd seen. Who was he? She hoped she would find out when she got to the yard.

Tilly untacked Magic. He hadn't sweated while they'd been working, so she was able to put his turn-out rug straight on. It was an extra thick one, especially for the cold weather.

'If anything will make you feel cosy and snug, Magic, this will.'

She'd bought it for him a couple of Christmases ago and it had lasted well, although it was looking a bit shabby now. Magic had a habit of rolling in the muddiest parts of the field.

'Maybe it's time to get you a new one,' she said. 'A horse as smart as you should have smart rugs to match.'

Magic gave a small nicker. She led him across to the feed room and gave him a handful of nuts, then headed down to the long field. On the way they passed Angela's dad, Jack Fisher. He was talking to a man Tilly didn't recognise. Beside them was the magnificent bay.

'Morning, Tilly,' Jack called.

'Hi.'

'Good to see Magic's rugged up. It's going to be a cold winter, this one. Martin here says the forecast is for snow this week.'

'Is he yours?' said Tilly, unable to take her eyes off the beautiful horse. He was slightly bigger than Magic, about 16.2hh,

Tilly guessed, and his coat was like copper satin. He stood proudly. Tilly thought he had a wise expression on his face. She wondered what sort of things he'd done in his life. His ears were keen and alert.

'Ah, sorry, Tilly,' said Jack. 'I haven't introduced you. This is Royal Flame. And this is Martin, an old friend of mine. Martin's off to Greece for Christmas.'

Martin smiled.

'Yes, I'm escaping the cold for a few months. Luckily, Jack's agreed to help me out.'

'We're looking after Royal Flame while he's away,' explained Jack. 'So you'll have plenty of time to get to know him. He's a very special horse.'

'I hope he doesn't mind the cold weather!' said Tilly.

'Oh, Royal Flame isn't fazed by anything,' said Jack.

'He's an ex-police horse,' said Martin proudly. 'He's the bravest animal I know. We worked together in the Mounted Police force for years. He's certainly earned his retirement.'

Tilly smiled. The thought of an ex-police horse coming to stay at Silver Shoe was exciting. She remembered the amazing stunts she'd seen at Olympia – twelve police horses jumping through flaming hoops and performing a musical ride.

Tilly looked at Royal Flame. He stared back, his black eyes shining. She couldn't wait to get to know him properly.

Two

That afternoon, Tilly and her friends, Mia and Cynthia, gathered in the club room to help Angela plan the Silver Shoe Christmas party. It was held every year and everyone looked forward to it. All the horse owners, riding school students, and friends of Silver Shoe were invited, including the farrier, the vet, and the people who supplied hay and feed.

The horses were included in the festivities, of course. They got to eat their own version of Christmas pudding. It was basically a mix of all the things they liked to eat – carrots, apples, oats and a few sugar lumps.

The girls were sitting on the sofa. They each had a hot chocolate and there was a plate of Angela's homemade cinnamon cookies to share. Cynthia had a pen and clipboard on her lap. She had appointed herself note-taker. She liked to be very organised.

'With Silver Shoe so full, the guest list is going to be bigger than ever this year,' said Angela. 'We've got to make it extra special. Has anyone got any ideas?'

'Maybe we should have a theme?' said Cynthia.

'That's easy,' Mia replied. 'Christmas is our theme!'

'I mean, we could do something different, like have a colour scheme. I think everything should be purple and silver.'

'I'm afraid,' said Angela, 'that the Silver Shoe Christmas decorations are all varying colours, shapes and sizes, and we can't run to the expense of buying new ones. We'll have to make do.'

Tilly agreed. If there was ever spare money around, she thought it should be spent on things for the horses – not fancy decorations for a party that only happened once a year.

'We just need to make it lovely and Christmassy,' she said. 'We can do that for free.'

'We'll have a buffet of course,' said Angela. 'With mince pies and crackers.'

'We can sing carols,' said Mia, bursting into high-pitched singing. 'We wish you a merry Christmas . . . We wish you a merry . . .'

'Make it stop!' said Tilly, laughing.

'I think that might scare the horses!' said Angela, with a smile. 'What else?'

'We could collect holly and mistletoe from the forest to decorate the yard. And put fairy lights all around the stable block,' suggested Mia. 'That always looks pretty.'

'That reminds me, I should get some new fairy lights, a few of the bulbs have gone on the old set,' said Angela.

'What about roasting chestnuts?' said Cynthia.

'Mmm,' said Angela. 'I love those. That *is* a good idea. They make me feel really festive. Dad used to do them when I was little. I'm sure he'd do them again.'

'I hope it snows, like Jack's friend Martin said it would,' said Tilly. 'Then we'll have a proper winter wonderland.'

She pictured herself riding Magic across a snow-covered countryside, everything still and quiet and magical, Magic's silvery coat almost camouflaged by the white landscape. He was beautiful and sleek, the horse of her dreams. She was so lucky.

Tilly glanced out of the window. It wasn't snowing, but the sky looked heavy and white, as though snow was on its way. Then she noticed Royal Flame being led

across the yard by Duncan, Silver Shoe Farm's head boy. It struck her again what a noble-looking animal Royal Flame was. He walked with grace and dignity, holding his head high. He'd been at Silver Shoe for less than a day and already he seemed relaxed and sure of his surroundings.

'He's majestic, isn't he?' said Angela, joining her at the window.

'Yes,' said Tilly. 'And stunning.'

'My dad's known that horse for a long time. He's always talking about how special he is. It's quite a treat to have him staying with us. Apparently, he was one of the best known horses in the police force. He's seen some major action and been involved in some really important jobs – patrols, crowd control at big events, that sort of thing.'

'What sort of events?'

'Mostly football matches and demonstrations – situations where public order needs to be maintained. The big police horses are used to help get people to cooperate in the midst of all the noise and activity. I suppose their size is intimidating if you're on the ground.'

'I can't imagine how Magic would cope in a situation like that. He'd be terrified.'

'The Mounted Police horses go through a rigorous training process, Tilly – that's how they manage to stay calm. I read somewhere that the police like to work with half or three quarter bred horses. They combine the spirit of a thoroughbred and the strength and stability of a draught horse. It's important to have the right character. They have to be strong and steady enough to remain calm in any situation, but they also have to be smart and obedient.'

'Wow. Remember those police horses we saw at Olympia? I never realised how much work they did!' said Mia.

'Oh yes,' said Angela. 'The Activity Ride. It's world famous. They perform it at horse shows everywhere, to display the Mounted Branch's skill and training. I believe Martin and Royal Flame have done a few of those together. They select the most accomplished and committed horses and riders to take part. It's a real honour.'

'Are they the horses that jump through flaming hoops?' said Cynthia. 'I've always wanted to see them.'

Tilly nodded. The horses at Olympia had shown off all sorts of skills, but the most impressive had been the flaming hoops. Angela was right. It was going to be a treat having Royal Flame to stay for Christmas.

Three

On Sunday morning, Tilly and Mia got
ready to ride Magic and Autumn Glory
over to meet Tilly's brother, Brook, and
their friend, Cally, at Cavendish Hall.
They were planning to go for a hack.
It was to be their last ride all together
before Cally went to Dubai for two weeks
to spend Christmas with her parents.

As they tacked up, Tilly could feel the
bite in the air.

'I think the snow is finally on its way.

I saw it on the weather this morning. '

'I'm glad I wore my sheepskin-lined jodhpur boots,' said Mia. 'I hate riding with cold feet.'

'Me too,' said Tilly. She had her own secret weapon. She was wearing a pair of silk socks, a silk thermal top and silk glove liners to go under her riding gloves – a present from her mum and dad last Christmas. They were excellent for keeping out the cold without adding extra bulk.

She warmed Magic's bit in her hands.

'There. That's better,' she said, as she eased it into his mouth. 'I'm glad the farrier replaced your shoes the other day. I wouldn't want you slipping and sliding on frozen ground.'

She saw Duncan carrying a bucket of grit across the yard. He'd been spreading it everywhere to prevent the yard getting icy and dangerous.

'Take care, you two,' he called. 'Don't go too far if the weather starts to turn.

I don't want to have to rescue you from a snow drift!'

By the time Tilly and Mia reached the gates of Cavendish Hall, the first snowflakes were beginning to fall. The tall fir trees that surrounded the gates were the perfect backdrop.

'It's as if we're riding inside one of those snow-globe thingies!' said Mia.

'It's magical,' said Tilly. 'Look. I can see Brook and Cally. Hey, guys!'

Brook and Cally waved. They were waiting with their horses, Solo and Mr Fudge, and walking in small circles trying to keep warm. The horses, however, looked perfectly at ease. They both had quarter sheets on. Tilly thought they looked a bit like the exercise rugs that racehorses usually wore. The sheets were fitted under their saddles and covered their

backs so they wouldn't feel the cold.

'I could do with one of those,' said Mia. She had so many thick jumpers beneath her fleece-lined coat, she was twice her normal size.

'You look like a marshmallow!' said Cally. 'Can you actually move?'

'Not really,' said Mia. She wriggled up and down in the saddle. 'I'm finding it hard to ride with so many layers, but at least I'm warm.'

The others laughed. Mia always moaned about the cold, even in summer. Tilly was glad for her light silk thermals, which were keeping her snug but weren't interfering with her riding.

'Where shall we head for?' said Mia.

'Maybe we shouldn't go too far,' said Brook. 'In case the conditions get worse. What about the woodland path that goes around the back of the Cavendish Hall stables? It's a nice, easy hack.'

'And it will look really pretty in the snow,' said Cally. 'It's settling. I'm glad

I've seen this before I go to Dubai. It won't be very wintery there – I'll miss a proper traditional Christmas.'

'You'll miss the Silver Shoe Christmas party too,' said Mia. 'I can't believe it's the first time you won't be there! You can make it though, can't you, Brook?'

'Definitely.'

'It's going to be a good one this year,' said Tilly. 'Angela says it'll be the biggest yet. And we have a special guest.'

'Who's that?'

'Royal Flame. He's an ex-police horse. He belongs to a friend of Jack Fisher and he's staying at Silver Shoe for a month. You've got to see him. He's stunning.'

They set off along the woodland path. Magic seemed a little unsure of the snowflakes at first. He kept flicking his head and snorting as the snow tickled his nose. Tilly hoped the horses in the long field at Silver Shoe weren't bothered by the weather. She knew Royal Flame wouldn't be. He was in a stable. Having worked all his life, he wasn't used to being turned out during the winter, so Angela had said it wouldn't have been fair to change his routine while he stayed with them.

The delicate white flakes danced around and the only sound was the crackle of frozen leaves beneath the horses' hooves.

'It's beautiful,' Tilly said. 'Hey, we should take a photo.'

The four friends stopped and, one-by-one, coaxed their horse into a line.

It took a couple of tries to get close enough together, but eventually Tilly was able to take the picture. She got out her phone and leaned back in the saddle. She held it up so she could fit everyone in, including herself.

'Smile!' she said, as she framed the scene. 'Winter wonderland!'

Four

When Tilly and Mia arrived back at Silver
Shoe, Angela and Duncan were busy
making sure there was plenty of extra feed
for the horses to keep them fuelled through
the cold weather. Some of the horses were
wrapped up in their stables, but the ones
who preferred being turned out were cosy
in their winter rugs and very content with
the extra hay they had been given. They
also had the protection of the run-through
barn if they wanted shelter.

'Hi, girls,' said Angela.

'Hi, Angela.'

Tilly dismounted and wiped the snow from her riding hat. Underfoot, she could feel the crunch of the grit Duncan had put down.

'Nice ride?'

'It was lovely,' said Tilly

'You'd better get dry rugs on those two,' said Angela. 'It may be chilly, but they've still produced heat and sweat through their exercise. The quicker they're warm and covered up, the less likely they are to get a chill.'

'Okay,' said Mia.

'And I've just mixed a bucket of lukewarm water if you want to give them some,' added Duncan. 'In this weather I always add some hot water to the ice-cold stuff that comes from the outdoor tap. If it's too cold, it can sometimes discourage them from drinking. We don't want any of the horses getting dehydrated. After exercise you should always offer the horses water before they eat. If they drink too much straight after eating it can increase the risk of colic.'

'Thanks,' said Tilly, making a mental note. She knew how badly horses could be affected by colic. She remembered how frightening it had been when Magic had suffered a blockage in his stomach. She didn't want anything like that happening again.

She took the bucket from Duncan and led Magic over to the stables, where she tied him up. Mia and Autumn followed behind. Mia fetched their winter rugs from the tack room while Tilly gave them the water. She was pleased to see both horses drinking deeply.

She removed Magic's tack and wiped him down, then rubbed the flecks of damp mud from his legs, belly and face with a damp towel. Duncan had told them not to use the hose in the yard at the moment because it was so cold and he was worried about it freezing. As she was finishing, Angela came by.

'Could I ask a favour, Tilly? Most of
the horses are sorted now and I need to
go into town. The thing is, Royal Flame
hasn't been out today. He's a horse who
likes activity. I know it's cold but I was
wondering if you and Mia could take him
to the sand school and give him some

exercise. The lanes will be too hazardous with all the snow now.'

Tilly's eyes widened.

'We'd love to,' she said.

'Thanks, Tilly. I knew you'd see it as a treat rather than a chore.'

'Definitely!'

Tilly couldn't wait to see what it felt like to actually ride a horse like Royal Flame. It was a privilege. She imagined herself in a Mounted Police uniform, with Royal Flame standing in front of a noisy crowd, fearlessly keeping order. Even though she was only going to take him around the sand school at Silver Shoe, she felt a tingle of excitement.

Once Magic was settled, Tilly fetched Royal Flame from his stable and tacked him up, with Mia's help. As they were placing the saddle onto his back, they

noticed a scar on his shoulder. It had faded
but it was quite large.

'Oooh!' said Mia.

'I wonder how he got that?' said Tilly.

She gently ran her finger across the scar.
Royal Flame quivered slightly. He gazed at
Tilly intently. As she looked into his eyes,
she sensed an energy about him. He was
obviously eager to be ridden.

'You'd better take it easy, Tilly,' said
Mia. 'He's huge.'

'I'm not worried,' said Tilly. 'I think
he'll be as sturdy and sensible as anything,
won't you, boy? He's had so much training.'

'Let's get going,' she whispered.

Royal Flame bobbed his head and stood
perfectly still. He was poised and ready.
Tilly thought he was exactly the sort of
police officer she'd want to call if ever she
was involved in a tricky situation.

It was starting to get dark and
snowflakes tumbled through the deep
blue sky. Mia switched on the floodlights.
As the sand school lit up, Tilly led Royal
Flame inside, and went to the corner where
there was a mounting block. She heaved
herself up. He was bigger than other horses
she'd ridden so she had to swing her leg
high in order to clear his wide back, but
she managed it in one go. He wasn't much
taller than Magic, but he was considerably
broader. Mia helped to adjust the stirrups,
then they were ready.

Tilly took up the reins and nudged with her heel.

'Walk on,' she said.

Royal Flame responded immediately. He was strong. At first she could feel him pull and she had to resist the temptation to pull back. She knew she must feel quite different to him too, if he'd always be ridden by a man.

'How is he?' said Mia.

'Big. But amazing!' said Tilly.

Although Royal Flame was powerful, Tilly discovered that, true to his training, he was also obedient. As if he was back on duty, he obeyed her every command. She trotted him on and did a few circuits of the sand school.

'Looking good,' said Mia. 'How's his canter?'

'Let's find out!'

Tilly asked with her leg. She felt a strong forward thrust as Royal Flame sped up. They did two laps. It was rather uncomfortable.

'Whoa!' said Tilly, grateful when Royal Flame reacted instantly to her request to slow down. 'I don't think they have to canter much when they're on police duty.'

'You looked great, but he's strong, isn't he?' said Mia. 'Well done for keeping your cool! So, what's next? A flaming hoop?'

Tilly laughed and shook her head.

'I think that's enough for now. It's your turn.'

As Tilly dismounted, a little part of her couldn't help wondering how scary it would be to be surrounded by hoards of football fans.

'You must be very brave,' she whispered, stroking the scar on his shoulder and passing the reins to Mia.

Royal Flame gave a small, contented nicker. Tilly was glad. He'd obviously appreciated the exercise, and she hoped she'd get to ride him again soon.

Five

That evening, when Tilly got home she took a long, hot bath. Her mum had made toad-in-the-hole for dinner, one of her favourites. As they sat at the table, she told her parents and her little brother, Adam, all about Royal Flame.

'I could tell he wouldn't give me any trouble,' she said.

'It's a good job,' said her dad. 'Those horses have to face all kinds of scary situations. I saw the Mounted Police at the football yesterday. They were trying to control the crowds. A few people got rowdy and started shouting and throwing stuff. But the horses didn't even flinch. It was pretty impressive stuff.'

'It must be helpful for the officers to have that extra height, sitting up on horseback,' said Tilly's mum.

'It would certainly give them a better vantage point. They'd be at least three metres off the ground.'

'Do you think Royal Flame has ever solved any crimes?' said Adam.

'Maybe,' said Tilly, although she wasn't sure the horses actually did *that* sort of police work.

'Cool.'

Later, Tilly decided to email the snowy photo she'd taken of her friends to Chief Four Paws. Chief Four Paws was the leader of the Native American tribe that she and Brook had been in contact with, after they'd discovered their birth mum had stayed on the reserve.

Hi Chief Four Paws,

Here's a picture of Brook and me with our friends and our horses, enjoying the snow. It's very cold here, but we're looking forward to Christmas. How is life on the reserve?

Tilly

Next, she looked up the Metropolitan Police Mounted Branch. On their website, she read that horses had been used by the police since 1760. There were whole teams of people involved, all doing different jobs – trainers, saddlers, farriers, horsebox drivers and stable hands. Having had the chance to ride Royal Flame, Tilly wanted to find out about the special training that made him so steady and calm.

It sounded intensive. The website explained that the training was separated into different stages, red, amber and green – like a traffic light system. The red stage involved establishing the basics, like standing still, being calm and polite, and being loaded on and off horse-boxes. Then, at the amber stage, the horses would be introduced gradually to new environments and exposed to different noises, conditions and objects. Finally, for the green stage, the horses would do daily patrols, learn to cope with traffic and practise special exercises to help them move laterally within a crowd.

No wonder Royal Flame seemed so well-balanced and obedient, thought Tilly. She could hardly believe the amount of training he'd had. She wondered if he missed the action now he was retired.

Just then, her inbox flashed. She had two messages. The first one was from Chief Four Paws.

Hi Tilly,

Thanks for the photograph. It certainly looks as though you and your horses have fun together. It is cold here too. I'm attaching a photo of one of the horse herds on the reserve. As you can see, they are all huddling together to keep warm. But they don't really mind the cold weather. They're a very hardy breed and their coats grow thick in the winter. Enjoy your Christmas.

Chief Four Paws

Tilly opened the image. It filled her computer screen and she was immediately struck by how similar the horses – beautiful wild Mustangs – were to the one in the photograph she had of her birth mum. In the Chief's photo there

were at least twenty of them, gathered at
a watering hole. They were a mix of bay,
palomino and silver dapple.

She forwarded the photograph to Brook.
She knew he'd like to see it, because
it was another clue to their past. Then
she opened the second message. To her
surprise, it was from a magazine, about a
prize draw competition that she'd entered
ages ago. She'd sent in a photograph of
Magic, for the chance to win a horse safari
trip in Botswana, Africa.

She held her breath as her finger
clicked on the mouse. But when it opened,
she saw that it was just an information
message, letting her know her entry had
been received and that the draw would
take place soon.

'Oh, well.'

She sighed and sat back. She didn't
mind too much. There was already plenty
to look forward to – getting to know Royal
Flame, spending the school holidays with
Magic, and, of course, the Silver Shoe

Christmas party. Besides, if the prize draw hadn't been called yet, there was still a chance.

Six

Before Tilly knew it, the final week of term had arrived and the Silver Shoe Christmas party was set for the coming weekend. It was hard to concentrate on school work when there were so many exciting things going on, but most of her teachers relaxed and organised some fun activities.

On the evening of the party, Tilly made sure she was one of the first people there. Guests gathered in the yard for hot-spiced apple juice and mince pies. Most of the snow had thawed, but it was still cold.

The sound of laughter and chatter created a lovely warm atmosphere. Tilly wore a thick quilted gilet, with a woolly hat, scarf and gloves, which had a horseshoe pattern knitted into them.

'Who wants some roasted chestnuts?' Jack Fisher called. 'Get them while they're hot!'

He was cooking the chestnuts over a barbecue. They smelled delicious.

'Mmm. I'll try one,' said Mia.

She rushed over.

'Careful,' warned Jack. 'Don't hurry when there's a hot fire nearby. It's a windy evening. I'll have to be careful to put this thing out properly when we go inside. There you go.'

He handed her a little bag of chestnuts.

'And take some for Tilly too.'

Mia returned to where Tilly was standing near Magic's stable. Magic was cosy inside, wearing his big thick stable rug. He and the other horses bobbed their heads over the stable doors to watch the activity. It was a pretty scene. Angela had been concerned that the fairy lights wouldn't work, but barring a few dodgy ones, the rest twinkled and sparkled making everything look very festive.

'There are so many people, aren't there, Magic? I recognise that man from the Riding for the Disabled centre, where the little pony, Rusty, went. He's a friend of Angela's. And, look, there's Elizabeth from Waltham Grange. We went to her stables when we were looking for your horse, Mia. Remember? That man over there with the beard must be a friend of Jack Fisher's. I don't think he should be smoking in the yard...'

Mia couldn't speak. She had a mouthful of roast chestnuts.

Tilly wondered whether they should say something to the man. She was about to go over when Magic leaned forward and tried to nibble the chestnuts in her hand.

'Hey! Easy, boy, these aren't for you,' said Tilly. 'They'd be too hot for your mouth. But don't worry. Here comes

Tim, with Jack's horse-friendly Christmas pudding – your very own party treat!'

Tim hadn't been part of the Silver Shoe gang for long, but he'd quickly made friends with Tilly and Mia. He'd arrived in the early autumn, desperate for help with his naughty pony, Buttons. With a bit of help from everyone at Silver Shoe, Tim and Buttons had discovered carriage driving. They both loved it and Buttons was like a different pony.

'Hi, Tim.'

'Hi, guys,' he said, coming forward to stroke Magic's nose. 'Do your horses want some of this? Apparently it's full of oats and carrot and sugar beet and all sorts of good things.'

Tim was about to offer a piece to Magic, when he saw Magic was already helping himself – munching big chunks of it straight from the tray!

'Hey, greedy guts! That's for sharing with all the horses!'

'I guess he likes it,' said Mia, laughing. 'We'll have to tell Jack that his special recipe is a hit.'

Tilly smiled at Tim. His nose was glowing red in the cold.

'Do you want a hand giving out the rest?' she said. 'That's if Magic doesn't scoff it all first!'

'Sure,' said Tim.

One by one, they fed pieces of the pudding to the horses. As they worked their way along the stable block, they could hear the sound of Christmas music. Duncan had found an old Christmas Hits CD in the box of decorations and rigged up his sound system to play them outside.

Mia groaned. 'I've heard these songs SO many times! Every year! The same ones!'

Tilly didn't mind. Some of them were terrible, but she liked the way they added to the festive mood. She went over to Pickle's stable.

'Ho ho ho! Merry Christmas!' she said, as she held out her hand, palm flat, and allowed the little pony to sniff and bite her treat.

Pickle loved it and clearly wanted more when it was offered. So did Autumn Glory, Red Admiral, Lulabelle, Lucky, Rosie and Nimrod. But Tim's pony, Buttons, was the keenest of all.

'Whoa!' said Mia. 'He was so excited he nearly ate my glove too!'

'We mustn't forget Royal Flame,' said Tilly. 'I'll take some over to him now.'

Royal Flame was in the end stable. He was the only horse who hadn't taken much notice of the party action. Tilly guessed it was because he was used to big crowds, lights and noises. It wasn't anything new or surprising to him.

She called his name softly and he looked up at her. If he hadn't been interested in the party, he was certainly interested in saying hello. He stared for a moment then came towards her, with the same sparkle in his eyes that she'd seen at the sand school. She was glad.

'That's it, boy,' she whispered. 'Remember me? I've got a treat for you.'

She held her hand and offered him a piece of the pudding. He gave it a glance but didn't accept it.

'Not to your tastes, eh, boy? Oh, well. I'll have to let Jack Fisher know you're the only horse who isn't a fan.'

'Fan of what?'

Jack's voice came from behind her.

'Oh, hi, Jack. Royal Flame isn't too hungry for this pudding.'

'That doesn't surprise me. He's always been a fussy eater.'

Jack stroked Royal Flame's nose affectionately. Royal Flame nuzzled into his hand.

'I expect his diet and feeding regime in the Mounted Police was very strict,' he said. 'They really look after the horses they train. They have to be in tip-top condition for all that patrol work. I hear you gave him a turn in the sand school the other day? It's been ages since I've ridden him. How was he?'

'Amazing!' said Tilly, wide-eyed.
'He's so strong and confident.'

'He sure is. But he's had to be.
He's been in situations that would spook
even the boldest of horses.'

'Like what?'

Tilly was fascinated.

'Well, the most dramatic moment
Martin told me about was when they were
involved in a demonstration that got out

of control. Royal Flame received a wound to his shoulder, but he remained on the scene and continued to work. It wasn't until a Mounted Police stable hand came to assist that they realised he'd been injured. Luckily he made a full recovery. You can barely see the scar.'

Tilly's stomach tightened. The thought of horses being ill or wounded always upset her. She remembered the scar she'd seen on Royal Flame's shoulder. She reached up and stroked his neck.

'He's very brave,' she said.

'Yes,' said Jack. 'When Royal Flame retired, some of the senior officers described him as one of the bravest horses they'd ever had in the Mounted Police. That's quite an accolade.'

'I bet he deserved it,' said Tilly. She felt more in awe of Royal Flame than ever.

Seven

As the crowd began to grow, so did the party atmosphere. The chatter and laughter got louder and a box of crackers was shared. Soon, everyone was wearing silly party hats and telling bad jokes.

'Here's one for you,' said Tilly's little brother, Adam. He'd come to the party with Tilly's mum and dad. Mia, Cynthia and Tim's parents were there too.

Now, he stood in front of Tilly, Tim and Mia, reading the joke from a tiny rectangle of paper, a twinkle in his eye.

'Where do you take a sick horse?'

'I don't know,' said Tilly. 'Where do you take a sick horse?'

'To the horspital!'

'Terrible!' said Mia. 'Leave the jokes to me, eh?'

Suddenly Cynthia jumped between them all.

'Christmas kiss!'

She had a sprig of mistletoe and was trying to get people underneath it. For a second she held it over Tim and Tilly. They both smiled and blushed and shook their heads.

'Go and pester someone else,' said Tim.

'Try Duncan and Angela,' said Mia. 'It's about time those two got it together.'

'Where is Angela?' said Tim. 'I haven't seen her for a while.'

Just then, Angela emerged from the club room.

'Food is ready,' she announced. 'Come and help yourselves.'

The guests began to make their way inside. Tilly hung back and glanced at her watch. She was waiting for Brook to arrive. She didn't want him to miss all the fun.

'Is that him?' said Tim.

'Where?'

'At the gate now. I guess it's him, because he looks like you. A taller, older, male version of you.'

'Without the Pocahontas hair,' said Mia, playfully flicking Tilly's long plaits, which were dangling from beneath her woolly hat.

'Hi, Brook!' Tilly waved him over. 'You're just in time for some food.'

'Great,' said Brook. 'I'm starving. Sorry I'm late. I've had a nightmare getting Solo's coat clean. We did a heavy training session this afternoon and the ground was so slushy and muddy, he got covered in it!'

'I'm glad you made it,' said Tilly. 'You can relax now. You remember me telling you about Tim, don't you? He's Buttons' owner.'

Tim and Brook smiled and shook hands.

'How's the driving going?' said Brook.

'Well, thanks.'

'Tilly says you're really good.'

'Oh, I've only just started. But I'd like to see how far I can get and maybe try doing it competitively. You do lots of competing, don't you? Maybe you can give me some tips on how to handle pre-competition nerves?'

'Sure.'

They walked ahead. Tilly was pleased they were getting on so well. Mia linked arms and gave her a squeeze.

'I love Christmas,' she said. 'I hope the horses won't mind us leaving them out here while we all eat that delicious food indoors.'

'I'm sure they'll be fine,' said Tilly.

The club room was very crowded. There wasn't enough room for everyone, so guests spilled out on to the little patio at the back, which looked over the fields. A trestle table had been set up with plates of hot sausage rolls, chicken wings, mini pizzas, crisps and sandwiches. For dessert, there were more mince pies and chocolate yule log.

'Yum!' said Mia, squeezing her way towards the table.

'Save some for us,' said Brook.

It was nice to have everyone who had connections with Silver Shoe all in one place. The only person missing was Cally,

but Tilly knew she'd be having a good time with her parents in Dubai.

She looked about the room. Her own parents seemed to be having a lengthy conversation with Tim and Cynthia's mums – hopefully talking about how brilliant it was that their children spent so much time riding. Mia's mum and dad were chatting to Jack Fisher. The man from the RDA was talking to Stephen, the farrier. Brian, the vet, was talking to a couple of the Silver Shoe stable-hands and trying to impress them by juggling sausage rolls. Duncan and Angela were in a corner talking quietly. They did make a nice couple, thought Tilly. Where was Cynthia with her mistletoe now?

The Christmas songs continued to play in the background. None of the guests minded the cramped space or the cold patio. Everyone was enjoying the busy, bustling, merry occasion. So much so, in fact, that no one, not even Tilly, noticed what was going on in the yard.

A tiny spark had somehow carried into some bales of hay that were stacked next to the main stable block and they were beginning to smoulder. By the time Tilly and all the other guests were in the club room eating party food and having a good time, the smoulder had turned into fire and was spreading along the back wall of the stable block.

Eight

Tilly heard it first. She and Brook and Mia and Tim were standing by the buffet table, trying to see who could fit the most cheesy puffs into their mouth at once. She laughed a lot, until a sound unsettled her. It was a loud neigh.

'Did you hear that?'

'What?'

'The horses. Listen.'

Mia's eyes bulged as she chomped down on her mouthful of crisps.

'All I can hear is the terrible Christmas

music!' she said, swallowing.

'No, seriously,' said Tilly, distracted now. 'I heard neighing.'

'I heard it too,' said Tim. 'Shall we go and check everything's okay?'

'Yes, come on,' said Tilly.

They squeezed past the guests and made their way to the yard. The cold night sky twinkled with stars. The sound of neighing became louder and more insistent.

'Something's wrong,' said Tilly.

Immediately, they saw smoke billowing from the main stable block. It was the block where, amongst others, Magic, Buttons, Red Admiral, and Royal Flame were kept. The smell of burning hay was very strong.

Tilly's heart began to race.

'There's a fire!' she cried. 'Quick!'

She ran towards the stable. Her only concern was for the horses. Especially Magic. The thought of him trapped inside was sickening.

'Wait!' called Tim, pulling her back. 'Slow down! It's too dangerous!'

He forced her to stop and she caught her breath. She knew he was right. Although she was desperate to do something, anything, she knew she couldn't just rush in. It felt like torture, seeing the smoke and flames and hearing the sound of the horses, frightened and fussing. She had to do something to protect them.

'Have you got your phone on you?' said Tim.

'Yes.' Tilly reached into her pocket, her hands shaking.

'Right. You stay here and dial 999. I'll go back to the club room and alert everyone else.'

'Okay.'

'But don't go in that stable, Tilly. Promise me.'

'I promise.'

Tilly punched the three digits into her phone. Her legs had gone to jelly. What if Magic was badly injured? What if *any* of the horses were? What if it was too late? She couldn't bear it. As the call connected Tilly shuddered and took a deep breath.

'Emergency services. How can we help?'

'There's a fire. At my stables. Someone needs to come. Quickly!'

'What's your location?'

'Silver Shoe Farm, Whiteberry Way, on the outskirts of North Cosford. Please hurry. The horses are trapped and…'

Just then, a huge flame licked the roof of the building – vivid, angry orange against the dark sky. There was a horrible cracking sound, like splintering wood, followed by more frantic neighing and the trampling of hooves.

'It's getting worse!' cried Tilly, tearful and shocked. 'The horses – they're trapped!'

'Stay calm, young lady,' said the operator. 'You're doing really well. The emergency services are on their way now. I just need to take a few more details.'

The operator's tone was reassuring. She stayed on the line, asking Tilly questions. It wasn't long before Tim came outside with Duncan and Angela. The three of them ran towards Tilly, their faces stricken with panic. Tilly passed the phone to Angela so that she could give the operator more information.

'Well done,' said Tim, squeezing her shoulder.

Many of the other guests were now racing into the yard, including Tilly's dad. As soon as he reached Tilly, he gave her a big hug.

'I'm so scared, Dad. What's going to happen to Magic and the other horses? They're trapped! It's getting worse, the emergency services won't be here in time!'

She began to sob. He held her tight and stroked her hair.

'Try not to worry, Tiger Lil'. Everything's going to be okay. Look, Duncan and some of the others are opening one of the stables. They'll get the horses out, you'll see.'

Tilly lifted her head. She almost couldn't look, but if there was hope, she knew she had to. She saw Duncan, Jack, and Brian the vet pull open one of the doors. They stepped back immediately because of the intense heat. Thick smoke billowed out, but moments later, Brian went in, holding a cloth to his mouth, and emerged with Buttons. Buttons was jittery and whinnying, but as far as Tilly could make out he was unhurt.

Tim ran towards him and led him away. Tilly wanted to go after him, to say something about how relieved she was for them both, but she couldn't move. Her heart was aching.

She couldn't believe they'd all been
laughing and having fun while the horses
had been out here in the fire. She knew
she wouldn't take her eyes off the burning
stable block until Magic was safe.

The next stable along was Red
Admiral's. Jack wrestled the door open.

It was a few moments before Red
appeared. He was pulling and rearing.
It took all of Jack's skill to hold him steady
in order to move him away from the fire.
Finally Red was safe.

Duncan, Jack and Brian worked their
way along the line of doors as fast as they
could, coaxing the horses out one by one.
When eventually they came to Magic's
door, Tilly held her breath. She waited.
She prayed Magic would walk through
the smoky, dark mouth of the doorway
unscathed. It seemed like an eternity
went by.

But nothing happened.

Nine

'Why isn't he coming out?' she cried, pressing her face into her dad's chest.

'They're trying, Tiger Lil'. Duncan's gone in. I'm sure he's okay. There's no reason he'll be any more affected than any of the others. Calm down. You'll need to reassure him when you see him, so just try not to get too agitated.'

Tilly brushed her plaits away from her ears. It was hard to hear over the shouts and the fire, but nonetheless, she recognised

Magic's neigh. Tilly would have known it anywhere. Relief flooded through her.

Suddenly, Duncan reappeared. He was coughing.

'I need some help,' he called.

Tilly heard the panic in his voice.

'What's wrong?' she cried.

'Magic won't budge. He's too frightened. It's the fight-or-flight reflex. And he's fighting. He won't let me near him. It's like a furnace in there and it's thick with smoke. If we wait much longer, it'll be too late. I need some muscle power to pull him out! Fast!'

Just then, the sound of sirens wailed in the distance.

'They're on their way!' called Jack. 'We've got to keep trying until they get here. Brian, you help Duncan, I'll get Royal Flame.'

The siren grew louder, until the flashing blue lights were visible in the lane. The huge vehicles pulled into the yard. But for Tilly, it wasn't quick enough.

She broke away from her dad's embrace.
If anyone could calm Magic now, she knew
it was her. She had to go to him.

'NO!' her dad shouted. He pulled her
back, just as Tim had.

'I know you love Magic and I know you want to help him, Tiger Lil', but I can't let you go in there! Leave it to the experts.'

His voice was shaking. He was almost crying.

'Please, Dad! Magic needs me!'

'It's just too dangerous. I'm sorry.'

Suddenly, there was a cheer. Tilly looked up and saw that Jack had managed to get the last stable door open. It belonged to Royal Flame. Tilly was amazed. While all the other horses had been distressed, he barely seemed to register the chaos around him. She'd forgotten what a highly-trained, fearless horse he was. She couldn't help but stare.

As Jack led Royal Flame past the door of Magic's stable, Tilly noticed his tail twitch. Royal Flame's ears pricked and he gave a whinny.

Duncan had an idea. 'Why don't we try leading Royal Flame into Magic's stable? Magic might follow him out.'

'It's worth a try,' said Jack.

At last, little by little, and with Duncan and Jack's encouragement, she saw Magic emerge from the smoky stable behind Royal Flame. Tilly could see from Magic's posture how terrified he was. His ears were pinned back and he was baring his teeth. For a moment she was reminded of the neglected horse she'd first discovered on the roadside in North Cosford. Hardly daring to breathe, she watched as Magic followed Jack and Royal Flame to the middle of the yard.

The moment Magic was clear from danger, Tilly ran towards him. She threw her arms round his neck and cried, but this time, they were tears of relief.

The firemen wasted no time. They sprang into action, unwinding their hoses and running towards the burning stable block. One of them stopped to talk to Angela. He wanted to make sure there were no people or horses trapped inside.

'No,' Angela said, sounding shaken and tired. 'We had a few scary moments but we managed to get all the horses out safely – with a bit of help from one of our visitors.'

She glanced across at Royal Flame. The fireman nodded.

It took a long time before Tilly became aware of the activity that surrounded them. All she could think about was Magic and how she'd nearly lost him. Brook, Tim and

Mia came to see if she was okay, while Duncan and Angela talked to the police. Jack Fisher was with Tilly's mum and dad. She heard them remarking on Royal Flame's bravery.

'It's because horses are herd animals,' explained Jack. 'They look for a leader and Royal Flame has that leadership quality by the bucketload. His presence gave Magic the reassurance he needed, more than either Duncan or I could. Instinct told him to follow.'

'Royal Flame is quite a horse,' said Tilly's dad. 'I don't know what we'd have done without him.'

'Ah,' said Jack proudly. 'That's police horses for you.'

He patted Royal Flame on the back.

'He's a perfect example of what a horse can achieve. All those skills he gained with the police force haven't left him. He's special. He'll always be special.'

Tilly smiled. She wholeheartedly agreed.

She rested her head on Magic's shoulder. She could feel each fibre of his smooth grey coat against her cheek, and as she stroked him she remembered all the times she'd groomed him, all the times she'd taken him on long hacks through the countryside, all the times they'd jumped together, and all the wonderful moments they'd shared. She couldn't imagine a life without him. Now, thanks to Royal Flame, and Duncan, Jack, Brian and everyone else, she wouldn't have to.

Ten

As Tilly went to bed that night her mind was full of the events of the evening. She lay awake worrying about the damage to the stable block and how they'd manage the horses until it was repaired. She forced herself to concentrate on her relief and happiness that Magic and the other horses were safe. Eventually, she drifted off, but as soon as she woke up the next day, Tilly was desperate to go back to Silver Shoe. She didn't want breakfast or a shower or anything. She just wanted to see Magic.

'Come on, Tiger Lil'. I'll drive you over,' said her dad.

Tilly could tell he was keen to see Magic too. He didn't know much about horses, but he knew what they meant to Tilly. And in many ways, Magic was now one of the family.

On the way, Tilly checked her phone. There were messages from Brook, Tim and Mia, all talking about the fire and how glad they were that Magic, Autumn and Buttons were safe. Tilly replied:

ON MY WAY 2 SS NOW. CAN'T WAIT 2 C MAGIC
+ GIVE HIM A BIG HUG. C U SOON. XX

As they pulled into the yard, a strong smell of smoke lay heavy in the air and Tilly suppressed a shudder as she remembered everything that had happened. The stable block looked strangely lifeless, with its blackened beams and empty stalls.

'What a mess!' said Tilly's dad.

Angela, Jack and Duncan were clearing up. They all looked exhausted and stressed.

'Hi, Tilly,' said Angela. She stopped to give her a quick hug. 'Are you okay now? What a horrible experience. Magic's doing well though. We moved him into the big barn for the night with Royal Flame and the others.'

'Can I see him?'

'Of course.'

Angela led Tilly across the yard.

'The vet's checked all the horses,' she explained. 'Magic and a few of the others have suffered a bit from smoke inhalation, but there won't be any lasting damage. We need to make sure they get plenty of rest until they're fully recovered. And, of course, they've had a bad fright. They're pretty jumpy and they'll need lots of comfort and reassurance.'

'I can give them that,' said Tilly.

Tilly, her dad and Angela approached the barn. Magic bobbed his head over one of the doors and began to quiver. Royal

Flame appeared beside him.

'They're both pleased to see you,' said Angela.

Tilly smiled. She couldn't even begin to describe how pleased she was to see them. She kissed Magic's head and stroked his velvety nose, then stroked Royal Flame's.

'How about a groom?' she said.

Magic always found being brushed relaxing and enjoyable. It seemed like the perfect way to give him a bit of pampering. It would also help get rid of the smell of smoke from his coat. Royal Flame pricked his ears.

'You too,' said Tilly. 'I won't leave you out. You've done such a good job looking after Magic.'

While Tilly's dad helped the others clear up, Tilly led Magic and Royal Flame out into the yard, tied them, and started work on her grooming. She took her time. When she'd finished with Magic, she started on Royal Flame. He seemed to enjoy it just as much as Magic. She made sure she collected the stray tail-hairs then she twiddled them into a bracelet. She wanted to give it to Jack Fisher. She'd sensed a special bond between those two, and after last night it seemed right that Jack should have something to link him to Royal Flame.

A little while later, Jack appeared.

'I thought I'd find you here.'

'Hi. I've just finished grooming Magic and Royal Flame. Magic seems much calmer now.'

'Must be Royal Flame's good influence.'

'And, um, by the way,' Tilly said, stepping forward. 'I made you this.'

She gave Jack the bracelet she'd made from Royal Flame's tail.

'I know how much you respect him,' she explained. 'This will remind you of his bravery during the fire, and yours too.'

'Oh, Tilly. That's so thoughtful of you. He really is one of the greatest horses I've ever met. I'd be honoured to wear his bracelet.'

He tied it around his wrist and held it up to the light.

'I feel like I'm one of the gang now. For a while I was thinking everyone had one of your horsehair bracelets except me!'

As he said this, Royal Flame gave a nicker.

'That's right, boy.'

'It's my way of saying thank you,' said Tilly. 'For helping with Magic last night. If you hadn't, well . . .'

'Don't thank me,' said Jack. 'It was Royal Flame who encouraged him to leave the stable. I'm just glad Magic and the rest of the horses are safe. But that's the last time I do any chestnut roasting in the yard, I can tell you. I can't help feeling responsible for the fact that the fire started in the first place. I really thought I'd put the fire out properly when I'd finished roasting those silly chestnuts. The fire brigade aren't sure what caused it yet but they think maybe a spark carried into the hay barn, or else it could have been Angela's old fairy lights getting too hot. They found a cigarette butt too, but I just can't think where that would have come from. It's going to take weeks for that stable block to dry out and then we'll have a lot of work to get it restored.'

Tilly racked her brains for something to say to make him feel better. Suddenly, from nowhere, she remembered the man she'd seen earlier in the evening.

'Jack,' she said. 'There was a man here last night I didn't recognise. He was smoking and I thought he shouldn't have been doing it in the yard, but I didn't like to say anything . . .'

'Oh, you mean Alf!' said Jack. 'That man! I've warned him about smoking in the yard before! He's just too set in his ways.'

Tilly looked confused.

'Alf lives down the road,' explained Jack. 'His wife was a real horse lover, always used to come and visit, but she died late last year. Alf doesn't know much about

horses but he enjoys the company – that's
why we invite him. He'll be devastated
when he finds out. Oh dear.'

He looked down and frowned.

'Don't worry,' said Tilly. 'We'll all help
get things back to normal.'

She reached up and stroked Royal
Flame's ears. He leaned forward and rested
his head on her shoulder.

'He likes you,' said Jack. 'Watch out,
Magic! You have competition.'

Magic pressed his nose to Tilly's other
shoulder.

Tilly smiled and gave both Magic and

Royal Flame a gentle pat.

'I've said it before but I think you've got a great instinct for horses, Tilly,' said Jack. 'No wonder those two horses adore you.'

Suddenly Royal Flame dipped his nose towards Tilly's pocket. He'd obviously spied the carrots she'd bought for them.

'I think they like me because I give them their favourite treats!' she said.

Jack managed a small chuckle.

'Somehow, I think there's more to it than that,' he said, with a wink.

Tilly looked at Magic and Royal Flame, and as they looked back at her, she knew Jack was right. There was so much more.

Pippa's Top Tips

When riding, always try to stay focused. It's important for you and your horse to learn to ignore any distractions, especially if you're preparing for competitions.

Flat work is the best way to improve your riding. It will help your horse to strengthen up, and become better educated, balanced and well-mannered.

If you're riding on slippery roads, make sure your horse's shoes have been replaced recently so that he doesn't slip about and risk injury. Don't ride on the roads if they are icy.

Always grit icy yards – not just for your own safety, but for the horses' safety too.

If your horse is clipped and goes out in the field during the cold weather, make sure he wears a correctly fitting turn-out rug.

If your horse is clipped, he might need to wear an exercise sheet when you go out hacking, particularly if it is very cold.

Horses use a lot of energy in the winter trying to keep warm, so make sure you give them more hay if they need it, especially if there is snow on the ground.

Don't go out hacking if you feel the weather conditions are going to be unsafe.

If your horse's water is too cold, it might discourage him from drinking. Mix some hot water with the ice-cold water that comes from the tap so he doesn't become dehydrated.

After exercise, always offer your horse water before he eats. If he drinks too much straight after eating, it can increase the risk of colic.

Glossary

Hacking (p.12) – Riding in the country for pleasure.

hh / hands high (p.15) – Horses and ponies are measured in 'hands', a hand is 4 inches or 10.16 cm.

Mounted Police (p.17) – Police men and women who patrol on horseback. The height and weight advantage of horses mean that they are often used to help control crowds in cities.

Farrier (p.19) – Another name for a blacksmith. A specialist who takes care of horses' hooves, including hoof trimming and shoeing.

Thoroughbred (p.25) – Tall, slim, athletic horse used in racing and other equestrian sports.

Draught horse (p.25) – A large horse bred for hard, heavy tasks such as ploughing and farm labour. Draught horses tend to be strong and patient with a docile temperament.

The Olympia Horse Show (p.25) – Annual championship for international show jumping, held at the Olympia exhibition centre in London at Christmas-time. It has a Christmas pantomime spirit to it, with various displays and forms of equestrian enterntainment.

Colic (p.37) – Colic is, essentially, a stomach ache, but in horses it can range from mild to life threatening, so if your horse is showing any signs of stomach pain, such as kicking at his stomach or trying to roll a lot, call your vet straightaway.

Mustang (p.47) – A free-roaming horse of the North-American West.

Palomino (p.51) – A coat colour in horses, consisting of a creamy gold coat and white mane and tail.

Riding for the Disabled (p.55) – A charity dedicated to improving the lives of thousands of disabled people through education, therapy, fun and horse riding. For more information, visit www.rda.org.uk.

Points of a Horse

1. poll
2. ear
3. eye
4. mane
5. crest
6. withers
7. back
8. loins
9. croup
10. dock
11. flank
12. tail
13. tendons
14. hock joint
15. stomach

16. elbow
17. heel
18. hoof
19. coronet band
20. pastern
21. fetlock joint
22. cannon bone
23. knee
24. shoulder
25. chin groove
26. nostril
27. muzzle
28. nose
29. cheekbone
30. forelock

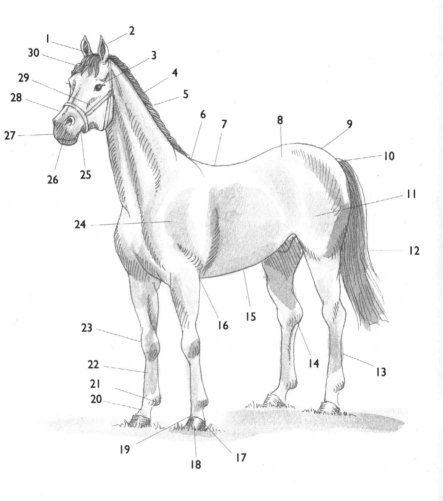

103

Pippa Funnell

"Winning is amazing for a minute, but then I am striving again to reach my next goal."

I began learning to ride when I was six, on a little pony called Pepsi.

When I was seven, I joined my local Pony Club – the perfect place to learn more about riding and caring for horses.

By the time I was fourteen and riding my first horse, Sir Barnaby, my dream of being an event rider was starting to take shape.

Two years later, I was offered the opportunity to train as a working pupil in Norfolk with Ruth McMullen, the legendary riding teacher. I jumped at the chance.

In 1987, Sir Barnaby and I won the individual gold together at the Young Rider European Championships, which was held in Poland.

Since then, hard work and determination have taken me all the way to the biggest eventing competitions in the world. I've been lucky and had success at major events like Bramham, Burghley, Badminton, Luhmühlen, Le Lion d'Angers, Hickstead, Blenheim, Windsor, Saumur, Pau, Kentucky – and the list goes on…

I married William Funnell in 1993. William is an international show jumper and horse breeder. He has helped me enormously with my show jumping. We live on a farm in the beautiful Surrey countryside – with lots of stables!

Every sportsman or woman's wildest dream is to be asked to represent their country at the Olympics. So in 2000, when I was chosen for the Sydney Olympics, I was delighted. It was even more special to be part of the silver medal winning team.

Then, in 2003, I became the first (and only) person to win eventing's most coveted prize – the Rolex Grand Slam. The Grand Slam (winning three of the big events in a row – Badminton, Kentucky and Burghley) is the only three-day eventing slam in the sporting world.

2004 saw another Olympics and another call-up. Team GB performed brilliantly again and won another well-deserved silver medal, and I was lucky enough to win an individual bronze.

Having had several years without any top horses, I spent my time producing youngsters, so it was great in 2010 when one of those came through – Redesigned, a handsome chestnut gelding. In June that year I won my third Bramham International Horse Trials title on Redesigned. We even managed a clear show jumping round in the pouring rain! By the end of 2010, Redesigned was on the squad for the World Championships in Kentucky where we finished fifth.

Today, as well as a hectic competition schedule, I'm also busy training horses for the future. At the Billy Stud, I work with my husband, William, and top breeder, Donal Barnwell, to produce top-class sport horses.

And in between all that I love writing the *Tilly's Pony Tails* books, and I'm also a trustee of World Horse Welfare, a fantastic charity dedicated to giving abused and neglected horses a second chance in life. For more information, visit their website at www.worldhorsewelfare.org.

Acknowledgements

Three years ago when my autobiography was published I never imagined that I would find myself writing children's books. Huge thanks go to Louisa Leaman for helping me to bring Tilly to life, and to Jennifer Miles for her wonderful illustrations.

Many thanks to Fiona Kennedy for persuading and encouraging me to search my imagination and for all her hard work, along with the rest of the team at Orion. Due to my riding commitments I am not the easiest person to get hold of as my agent Jonathan Marks at MTC has found. It's a relief he has been able to work on all the agreements for me.

Much of my thinking about Tilly has been done out loud in front of family, friends and godchildren – thank you all for listening.

More than anything I have to acknowledge my four-legged friends – my horses. It is thanks to them, and the great moments I have had with them, that I was able to create a girl, Tilly, who like me follows her passions.

Pippa Funnell
Forest Green, February 2009

For more about Tilly and
Silver Shoe Farm – including pony tips,
quizzes and everything you ever wanted
to know about horses –
visit www.tillysponytails.co.uk

Look out for

Pippa Funnell: Follow Your Dreams

Pippa Funnell as you've never seen her before.

Get to know Pippa – her loves, her hates, her friends, her family. Meet her beautiful horses, and take a sneaky peek at life on her gorgeous farm. Find out how she prepares for important competitions, trains and cares for her horses, and still has the time to write *Tilly's Pony Tails*.

And discover how, with hard work, passion and determination, you too can follow your dreams, just like Pippa.

978 1 4440 0266 9

£6.99

the
orion star

Sign up for **the orion star**
newsletter to get inside information
about your favourite children's authors
as well as exclusive competitions and
early reading copy giveaways.

www.orionbooks.co.uk/newsletters

Orion
Children's Books